The Escape of the Deadly Dinosaur:
USA

Join Secret Agent Jack Stalwart

on his other adventures:

The Search for the Sunken Treasure: **AUSTRALIA**

The Mystery of the Mona Lisa: **FRANCE**

The Secret of the Sacred Temple: **CAMBODIA**

The Escape of the Deadly Dinosaur: USA

Elizabeth Singer Hunt

Illustrated by Brian Williamson

RED FOX

THE ESCAPE OF THE DEADLY DINOSAUR: USA

A RED FOX BOOK 978 1 862 30122 1

First published in Great Britain by Chubby Cheeks Publications Limited
Published in this edition by Red Fox,
an imprint of Random House Children's Books

Chubby Cheeks edition published 2004
This edition published 2006

7 9 10 8 6

The Random House Group Limited supports The Forest Stewardship Council (FSC),
the leading international forest certification organisation. All our titles
that are printed on Greenpeace approved FSC certified paper carry
the FSC logo. Our paper procurement policy can be found at:
www.rbooks.co.uk/environment.

 Mixed Sources
Product group from well-managed
forests and other controlled sources
www.fsc.org Cert no. TT-COC-2139
© 1996 Forest Stewardship Council
FSC

Set in Meta, Trixie, American Typewriter, Luggagetag,
Gill Sans Condensed and Serpentine.

Red Fox Books are published by Random House Children's Books,
61–63 Uxbridge Road, London W5 5SA,
A Random House Group Company

Addresses for companies within The Random House Group Limited
can be found at:
www.randomhouse.co.uk/offices.htm

THE RANDOM HOUSE GROUP Limited Reg. No. 954009
www.**kids**at**randomhouse**.co.uk

A CIP catalogue record for this book is available from the British Library.

Printed and bound in Great Britain by
Cox & Wyman Ltd, Reading, Berkshire

For Catherine, Darcy, Patricia and Toni

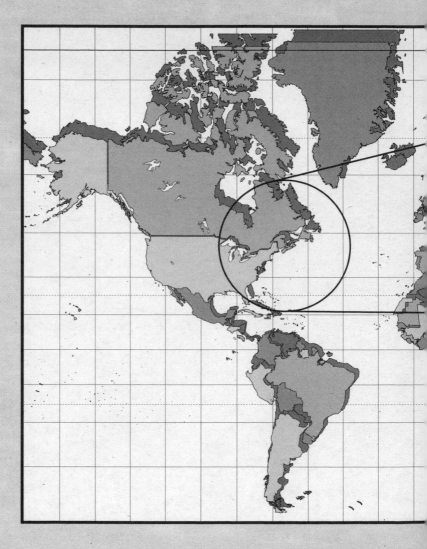

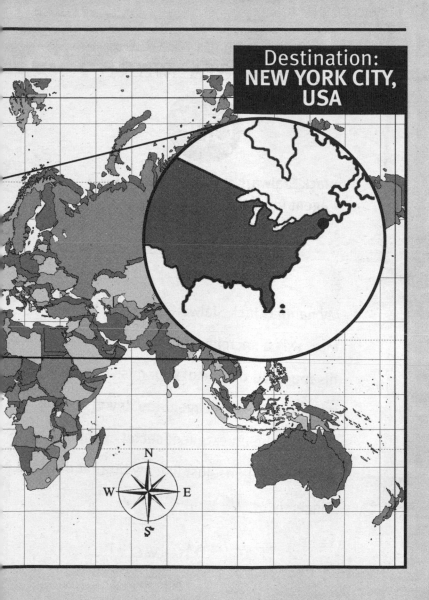

Destination:
NEW YORK CITY, USA

GLOBAL PROTECTION FORCE FILE ON
JACK STALWART

Jack Stalwart applied to be a secret agent for the Global Protection Force four months ago.

My name is Jack Stalwart. My older brother, Max, was a secret agent for you, until he disappeared on one of your missions. Now I want to be a secret agent too. If you choose me, I will be an excellent secret agent and get rid of evil villains, just like my brother did. Sincerely,

Jack Stalwart

HIGHLY CONFIDENTIAL

Jack Stalwart was sworn in as a Global Protection Force secret agent four months ago. Since that time, he has completed all of his missions successfully and has stopped no less than twelve evil villains. Because of this he has been assigned the code name 'COURAGE'.

Jack has yet to uncover the whereabouts of his brother, Max, who is still working for this organization at a secret location. Do not give Secret Agent Jack Stalwart this information. He is never to know about his brother.

Gerald Barter

Gerald Barter
Director, Global Protection Force

THINGS YOU'LL FIND IN EVERY BOOK

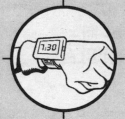

Watch Phone: The only gadget Jack wears all the time, even when he's not on official business. His Watch Phone is the central gadget that makes most others work. There are lots of important features, most importantly the 'C' button, which reveals the code of the day – necessary to unlock Jack's Secret Agent Book Bag. There are buttons on both sides, one of which ejects his life-saving Melting Ink Pen. Beyond these functions, it also works as a phone and, of course, gives Jack the time of day.

Global Protection Force (GPF): The GPF is the organization Jack works for. It's a worldwide force of young secret agents whose aim is to protect the world's people, places and possessions. No one knows exactly where its main offices are located (all correspondence and gadgets for repair are sent to a special PO Box, and training is held at various locations around the world), but Jack thinks it's somewhere cold, like the Arctic Circle.

Whizzy: Jack's magical miniature globe. Almost every night at precisely 7:30 p.m., the GPF uses Whizzy to send Jack the identity of the country that he must travel to. Whizzy can't talk, but he can cough up messages. Jack's parents don't know Whizzy is anything more than a normal globe.

The Magic Map: The magical map hanging on Jack's bedroom wall. Unlike most maps, the GPF's map is made of a mysterious wood. Once Jack inserts the country piece from Whizzy, the map swallows Jack whole and sends him away on his missions. When he returns, he arrives precisely one minute after he left.

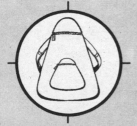

Secret Agent Book Bag: The Book Bag that Jack wears on every adventure. Licensed only to GPF secret agents, it contains top-secret gadgets necessary to foil bad guys and escape certain death. To activate the bag before each mission, Jack must punch in a secret code given to him by his Watch Phone. Once he's away, all he has to do is place his finger on the zip, which identifies him as the owner of the bag and immediately opens.

THE STALWART FAMILY

Jack's dad, John

He moved the family to England when Jack was two, in order to take a job with an aerospace company. As far as Jack knows, his dad designs and manufactures aeroplane parts. Jack's dad thinks he is an ordinary boy and that his other son, Max, attends a school in Switzerland. Jack's dad is American and his mum is British, which makes Jack a bit of both.

Jack's mum, Corinne

One of the greatest mums as far as Jack is concerned. When she and her husband received a letter from a posh school in Switzerland inviting Max to attend, they were overjoyed. Since Max left six months ago, they have received numerous notes in Max's handwriting telling them he's OK. Little do they know it's all a lie and that it's the GPF sending those letters.

Jack's older brother, Max

Two years ago, at the age of nine, Max joined the GPF. Max used to tell Jack about his adventures and show him how to work his secret-agent gadgets. When the family received a letter inviting Max to attend a school in Europe, Jack figured it was to do with the GPF. Max told him he was right, but that he couldn't tell Jack anything about why he was going away.

Nine-year-old Jack Stalwart

Four months ago, Jack received an anonymous note saying: 'Your brother is in danger. Only you can save him.' As soon as he could, Jack applied to be a secret agent too. Since that time, he's battled some of the world's most dangerous villains, and hopes some day in his travels to find and rescue his brother, Max.

DESTINATION:
New York City
USA

New York City is located on the continent of North America

•

There are fifty states in the United States of America

•

New York City is in the state of New York

•

New York got its name from the British, who named it after the Duke of York

•

New York City is also known as 'the Big Apple'

More than eight million people live in the city

•

Most of the streets in New York City cross each other at right angles

•

New York City is home to the Empire State Building, Times Square and the Statue of Liberty

THE ALLOSAURUS:

Everything You Ought to Know

by Lewis Porter

- Dinosaurs first appeared on Earth about 230 million years ago. (The first humanlike creatures appeared on Earth about three million years ago)

- The allosaurus appeared in the late Jurassic period, about 150 million years ago, and was one of the largest and most common predators

- It usually hunted in packs

- The name allosaurus means 'different lizard'. It's pronounced *al-o-saw-rus*

- A typical allosaurus was three metres high, ten metres long and weighed two tons

- The dinosaurs died out about sixty-five million years ago at the end of the Cretaceous period. No one knows why, but some people think it was because an asteroid hit Earth

SECRET AGENT GADGET INSTRUCTION MANUAL

Virtual Projection Camera:
Excellent for fooling bad guys into thinking you or something else is somewhere when you're not.

Just type in what you want to project and turn it on. An image will appear up to ten metres away with the right look, smell and sound. No one will know it's not for real.

Neutralizing Spray:
When you want the smell of you or something else to go away, the GPF's Neutralizing Spray is your best defence.

Just spray it on and within seconds any trace of your smell totally vanishes. Perfect when you've got meat-eating animals on your trail.

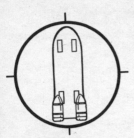

Flyboard: For help getting somewhere faster than your feet will take you. Looks like a skateboard but has two hydrogen jets mounted on the back. Just snap it together (it comes folded in half) and hop on. Push the word 'air' on your Watch Phone to make it fly, 'blades' to skate on ice, or 'wheels' to speed on the ground. After use, every secret agent must return it to GPF headquarters for hydrogen refuelling.

FLYBOARD PROTOTYPE: CURRENT RESTRICTIONS

Maximum lift height: 1 metre

Maximum speed: 25 miles per hour

Maximum usage time: 1 hour

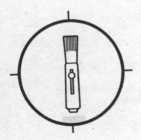

Goo Tube: Perfect for closing up bullet holes and making small repairs. Just lift up the tube with its expanding goo inside and press the ejector button. Instantly, sticky goo will come out and grow, closing the hole.

Chapter 1:
The Mysterious
Package

It was almost 7:15 p.m. and nine-year-old
Secret Agent Jack Stalwart was sitting at
his desk, doing his homework, when
there was a knock at his bedroom door.

'Who is it?' asked Jack.

'Just me, sweetheart,' said a kind voice
from the other side.

Jack got up from his desk, walked to his
door and opened it.

'Hi, Mum,' he said. 'What's up?'

'Just wanted to give you something,'
she said, handing him a package

wrapped in brown paper. 'It came for you in today's post.'

'Thanks,' said Jack, taking the package. It felt as if there was something hard inside.

'That Book of the Month club sure does send you quite a few books,' said Jack's mum, pointing to the sender's return address. Jack and his mum looked at the address together. It read: *Great Picks for a Fiver*, or GPF.

'Uh, yes,' said Jack nervously, worried his mum might catch on. 'They're great,' he added. 'They always send me just what I need.'

'Well,' he went on, holding the package close to his chest, 'I guess I'd better get on with my homework.'

'OK, dear,' said his mum as she walked away. 'Don't forget to clean your teeth before you go to bed,' she added.

Jack shut the door behind his mum and rushed over to his desk. He sat down and carefully unwrapped the package. Inside there was a book with a picture of a dinosaur on the front. It was entitled: *The Allosaurus: Everything You Ought to Know* by Lewis Porter.

The allosaurus, thought Jack. Why are they sending me a book about a dinosaur? And who is this guy, Lewis Porter? He doesn't work for the GPF.

Chapter 2:
The Big Apple

As Jack sat down to think about why the GPF would send him such a thing, a familiar whirring sound came from the corner of his room. It was Whizzy, Jack's miniature globe. Whizzy was starting to spin, as he did almost every night at precisely 7:30 p.m.

Jack was a secret agent working for the Global Protection Force, or GPF. His job was to travel the globe defeating evil people or things that threatened the world's most precious treasures. The GPF often sent Jack secret information critical to his next mission through the post. This time they had disguised it as a package from a children's book club.

When Jack was sworn in as a secret agent, the GPF gave him Whizzy. It was a clever way for them to send Jack details about the location of his next mission, because Jack's parents would never know that Whizzy was anything more than a normal globe. As Whizzy started to spin even faster, Jack knew it was only seconds until the GPF and Whizzy revealed where he would be travelling to next.

'Ahem!' Whizzy coughed. A huge jigsaw piece flew out of Whizzy's mouth and sailed past Jack and onto his desk. Whizzy let out a huge sigh of relief. Jack picked up the piece and carried it over to the Magic Map on his wall.

'This one is huge,' Jack said to himself. 'There are only a few countries in the world this size.'

The Magic Map on Jack's bedroom wall was spectacular. It was enormous, with over a hundred and fifty countries carved into it, each with its own shape and colour. Jack lifted the piece up to the first possible country. Immediately, the mystery piece slotted in.

'The United States of America!' he gasped with excitement. 'I'm going home! But I wonder where in the US I am going. There are fifty states, any one of which could need my help.'

Just then a small green light started to appear on the eastern side of the USA. Jack leaned into the map to get a better look. The light was coming from a tiny island inside the state of New York.

'New York City,' said Jack. 'Fantastic. I'd better grab my Book Bag before I go.'

Jack raced over to his bed and pulled out his Secret Agent Book Bag from underneath. He punched in the code of the day – A-P-P-L-E – and checked its contents. All the GPF's standard

gadgets were there, as well as the Flyboard and Picture Grabber. He locked his bag, tossing the straps over his shoulders, and rushed back to the Magic Map on his wall. The green light inside New York City grew brighter and brighter until it filled his bedroom.

When Jack was ready, he yelled, 'Off to New York City!' And with those words, the light flickered and burst, swallowing Jack into the giant map.

Chapter 3:
The Big Toe

When Jack arrived, he found himself
standing in the middle of a great hall. The
sun was shining down from the windows
near the ceiling, and the skeletons of
three massive dinosaurs towered above
him. Jack looked up – way up – at the
dinosaurs and wondered whether any of
the skeletons standing before him were
allosaurus, like in the book he'd received.

'Hmm. Hmm,' came a sound from
beside Jack.

He looked to his right and saw a skinny
man with wild, curly blond hair and

glasses standing next to him. The man seemed rather nervous, constantly shifting his feet and looking over each shoulder every couple of seconds. His glasses didn't fit very well, and he spent most of his time pushing them back up onto the bridge of his nose.

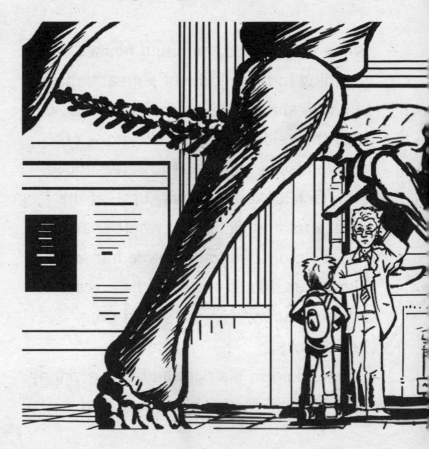

'You must be Jack,' he said, hugging a clipboard close to his chest. 'I'm Lewis. Lewis Porter. Thanks for coming,' he added, as he extended his hand to Jack and nodded hello. 'I'm the one who called the GPF. I am in charge of the dinosaur exhibit here at the museum.'

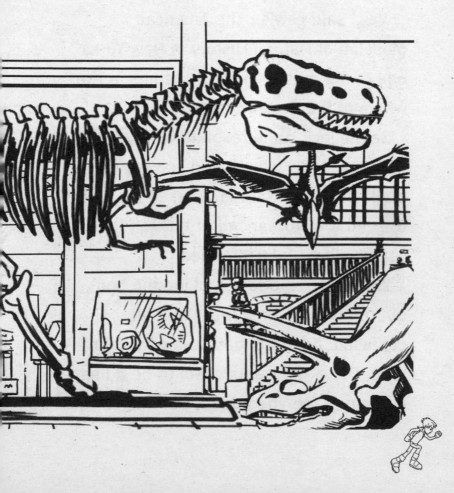

Jack remembered the name on the book from the GPF. The man standing in front of him was its author, Lewis Porter. The only question Jack had now was exactly which museum he was standing in. 'The museum?' asked Jack, fishing for more information.

'Yes,' said Lewis. 'The American Museum of Natural History in New York; one of the most famous museums in the whole of the United States.'

Before Jack could respond in any way, Lewis excitedly asked, 'Did you get the book on the allosaurus? I asked the GPF to send it to you ahead of time so that you would be fully informed.'

'Sure did,' said Jack, pulling the book out of his Book Bag. 'But I'm a bit confused. I don't understand why I am here. These dinosaurs seem to be doing all right to me,' he added, pointing to the three skeletons standing before him.

'Are you joking?' responded Lewis, who seemed genuinely shocked that Jack hadn't noticed what was wrong. 'It's so obvious!' he gasped, pointing to the smallest of the three dinosaurs. 'Someone has taken the hallux of this allosaurus!'

'The what?' asked Jack. He had never heard of a hallux before.

'The hallux!' said Lewis in exasperation, his arms flapping excitedly above his head. 'Come over here.' He yanked Jack towards the allosaurus. 'See!' Lewis pointed to where the toe should have been. 'The hallux – or first toe – of this dinosaur has been stolen!' he cried.

Jack looked at where the toe should have been. 'Are you sure it hasn't just fallen off?' he asked. He didn't want to be rude, but it would be a waste of time if the toe had simply fallen off and rolled underneath something on the floor.

'Things like this don't just fall off,' said Lewis. 'I know it doesn't look like much, but a missing anything on this dinosaur is a big deal. The allosaurus was one of the most ferocious carnivores of the Late Jurassic. Although it was smaller, it could bring down medium to large plant-eating dinosaurs, like the camptosaurus. It had an expandable jaw which enabled it to chomp down and eat big pieces of meat. It could carry its two-ton body on the strength of its muscular hind legs alone! This skeleton is almost one hundred and fifty million years old. That's why it's important to find the hallux, even if it is one of the skeleton's smaller bones.'

'When did you notice it was missing?' Jack asked.

'Last thing yesterday,' answered Lewis.

'Was there anyone strange lurking around the dinosaur?' asked Jack.

'Not really,' said Lewis. 'There were just some school kids on a field trip, like always.'

'Well then,' said Jack, 'the first order of business is to view the footage from your surveillance cameras. Perhaps I can sit in with your security guard while he looks at the tapes.'

'That's a great idea,' said Lewis. 'Let me take you to Hal, who is in charge of surveillance.'

'Thanks,' Jack said. 'And don't worry,' he added, trying to reassure Lewis. 'I'll find the dinosaur's toe.'

'I hope so,' Lewis said, sighing as he hugged his clipboard. 'Taking care of these dinosaurs is my life.'

Before leaving the room, Jack paused to look up at the gigantic skeletons once again. He thought about the TV show he'd recently seen; the one about the life and death of the dinosaurs. Jack shuddered to think what it would have been like to live among them, especially at the time of the allosaurus. The allosaurus was a relative of Tyrannosaurus rex and just as fearsome. Yes, Jack thought, he was glad the dinosaurs in front of him were a dead collection of bones.

'Jack,' said Lewis, waking Jack from his thoughts. 'Are you ready?' he asked.

'Sure thing,' said Jack, hurrying to catch up with Lewis, who by then had already left the hall.

Chapter 4:
The Security Meeting

Jack followed Lewis down to the depths of
the museum and into a large room filled
with high-tech surveillance equipment. In
the centre of the room was a man wearing
a security guard's uniform. He was sitting
in a chair in the middle of a circular desk
surrounded by at least ten television
screens and a panel of controls.

Each TV screen was linked to a digital
camera positioned in one of the
museum's rooms. All the security officer
had to do was push a button and the
image on the screen would change to

another from a different location. Not only could he watch events as they happened, he could record them. When Jack and Lewis entered the room, Jack noticed that the guard was looking at yesterday's tape.

'Hiya, Lewis!' said the man, a smile widening on his face. 'How's it hanging?'

'Uh. All right, Hal,' responded Lewis nervously. 'This is Jack Stalwart,' he said.

'He's going to help me find the allosaurus bone that went missing. Do you mind if he sits with you as you review yesterday's footage?'

'No problem. Come and sit down beside me,' said Hal as he pulled up a chair so that Jack could join him.

'Call me if you need me,' Lewis said before he left the room.

'Well,' said Hal as he punched some buttons, 'like I told Lewis, I didn't see anything unusual yesterday. Just some students passing through. Personally, I think Lewis is missin' a few screws – if you know what I mean. He spends way too much time with those bones. I've been looking at these tapes all morning and there's nothing on them to suggest anyone took a thing. Maybe Lewis was cleaning that bone and forgot to put it back or somethin'.'

'Maybe,' said Jack, 'but if Lewis is right, and the toe's been stolen, then we have a crime on our hands. Let's see what's on the video.'

Chapter 5: The Hook

Hal started the digital recording and a black and white moving record of the day before was played out before their eyes. They had watched the video for about an hour when Hal turned to Jack.

'See, I told you,' he said, pointing to the screen. 'Just a bunch of school kids on a field trip.'

Jack looked at the monitor. There was indeed an outing of school children whose teacher was showing them the magnificent dinosaur skeletons. As Jack studied the tape, he noticed something strange. One of the boys in the group lingered behind and reached out quickly towards the dinosaur. He then bent down to his school bag and put something inside before standing up to join the group again. At one point, he looked towards the camera.

'Wait,' said Jack to Hal. 'Can you rewind that section and play it again? But now,' he requested, 'can you play it one frame at a time?'

'You got it,' said Hal.

As Hal played the video in slow motion, Jack leaned in to get a closer look. This time he watched the boy carefully. As he watched, Jack couldn't believe his eyes. The boy had taken a long thin hook out of his jacket and yanked the toe off the dinosaur! He then put it in his school bag.

'I don't believe it!' said Hal. 'How did that get past me? I didn't see that happen.'

'It would have been hard to see,' said Jack, wrinkling his brow. 'This kid is clever and fast.'

Jack unlocked his Secret Agent Book Bag and took out the Picture Grabber. It was a slim, rectangular silver box that, when plugged into the back of a computer or TV, could take a still picture of whatever was on the screen and print it out in your hand.

'Now, can you pause the video just at the point where he turns towards the camera?' Jack plugged the Picture Grabber into the back of the monitor and pushed the 'grab' button. Instantly, it registered the image of the boy. Jack hit the 'print' button and a picture printed out from the side of the box.

'Do you know what school he goes to?'

asked Jack as he studied the boy's face.

'From the looks of the uniform, I'd say it was East Side Grammar School,' answered Hal. 'It's located at the intersection of 23rd Street and Park Avenue.'

'Great,' said Jack, putting the picture of the boy in his pocket. 'Thanks for your help. Looks like East Side Grammar School is my next stop.'

Chapter 6:
The Halls of Science

As Jack approached the towering steps of East Side Grammar, he paused for a moment to check his Watch Phone. It was just before 8:45 in the morning and, if it was anything like his school in England, classes were about to start.

Boys and girls were hurriedly climbing the steps. As they passed by Jack, he looked carefully at their red, green and grey clothes and compared them to the uniform on the boy from his picture. Yes, Jack thought, there was no doubt. The boy who took the bone from the museum was definitely a student at this school.

Trying to blend in with the others, he followed the students up the stairs and through the large red wooden doors. Amidst the clang of student lockers, Jack spied a sign that said PRINCIPAL'S OFFICE. There was an arrow on it pointing to the left. Following it, Jack came to a door with a name on it — PRINCIPAL JUDITH DANNER. He knocked twice.

A stern voice answered. 'Yes?'

Slowly, Jack opened the door. Sitting at the desk was a woman wearing a bright purple dress. 'Principal Danner?' he asked.

'Yes. Who's asking?' she replied, peering over her glasses and sizing up Jack. 'You don't look as if you attend East Side Grammar School.'

'No, Ma'am, I don't,' answered Jack. 'My name is Jack Stalwart,' he explained, showing his badge. 'I work for an

international organization called the Global Protection Force. I've been asked to trace the whereabouts of a dinosaur bone that was stolen from the Museum of Natural History. I have reason to believe that the person who took it attends this school.'

'One of my students?' said a surprised Principal Danner.

'Yes,' explained Jack, showing her the picture of the boy. 'I believe this student

took one of the toe bones from an allosaurus skeleton yesterday while on a field trip at the museum. I got this picture from the surveillance video.'

Principal Danner studied the picture. She shook her head. 'I can't believe it. It's Thomas Eberly. One of our finest science students. For the last two years, Thomas has won our school science fair. The entire school is waiting to view this year's entry. His project last year, 'The Survival of the Roach Through the Ice Age', won him top honours. He even took second prize at the state science-fair competition.'

'Do you know what class he's in right now?' asked Jack. 'I need to speak to him.'

'Unfortunately,' replied Principal Danner, 'Thomas isn't at school today. He's home sick with the flu.'

'I still need to speak to him,' said Jack. 'Do you have his address?'

'Normally, I wouldn't give out this information. But, as you work for the GPF . . .' Her voice trailed off as she looked for Thomas's information. 'Here it is,' she said, pulling a piece of paper out of one of her filing cabinets. 'He lives in an apartment on 33rd Street, where it crosses Park Avenue. Just ten blocks north of here.'

'Thanks, Principal Danner,' said Jack as he turned towards the door. 'I appreciate your help.'

As he left her office, Jack couldn't help but think about this boy named Thomas. He wondered if there was any link between this kid's science project and the missing toe bone.

There's only one way to find out, thought Jack as he hurried through the school and towards the steps outside.

Chapter 7:
The Experiment

As Jack bounded down the steps and onto Park Avenue, he looked out at the street before him. There was a swarm of yellow taxis lining the street and hundreds of people walking around. Horns were honking, people were talking loudly on their mobile phones and big delivery trucks were making stops in front of shop owners' basement doors. New York City, Jack was realizing, was definitely one of the busiest cities he'd ever seen.

Just then, the ground rumbled. Instinctively, Jack steadied his stance and

grabbed the
straps on his
Book Bag. He
looked through
the grating just
below him and saw
a silver train whizzing
past, under the pavement.
This was the subway – New
York City's underground railway – and
it was heading north through the city,
right underneath Jack's feet.

Jack carried on, up the ten blocks to
Thomas's apartment. He climbed the
stairs in front of the building and went
through a glass door. Stepping into a
small entrance hall, he found himself
facing another glass door. To his right was
a panel on the wall with a series of
names and buttons. Next to the button
marked 1B was the name Eberly. Jack

pushed it. A female voice came over the speaker.

'Hello?' it crackled.

'Hi,' said Jack. 'My name is Jack Stalwart. I'm here to see Thomas. Principal Danner gave me Thomas's address.'

There was a slight pause and then a click. The glass door leading into the building popped open. Jack pushed it further and walked inside, then followed the long hallway until he reached a door marked 1B. Before he could knock, the door was flung open and a friendly woman with an enormously toothy grin stood before him.

'Hi there!' she exclaimed. 'I'm Mrs Eberly. It's so nice of you to come and see Thomas, as he's sick and all. Come on in!'

Jack looked at the woman as she beckoned him inside. She was extremely tall and thin with curly red hair that hung just past her shoulders. It looked as though Jack had interrupted her in the middle of baking something; she was wearing an apron and had flour all over her hands.

'Come and sit down,' she added, pointing to a comfortable-looking sofa.

Her accent sounded like Jack's Aunt Millie's. Aunt Millie was Jack's father's sister. She was from Louisiana – one of the states in the southern part of the USA. She had visited Jack's family in England a few years ago.

'Would you like some juice or somethin'?' she asked Jack.

'Sure,' said Jack.

She walked over to the fridge and pulled out a carton of orange juice. As she poured a glass for Jack, she turned to him. 'I'm sorry,' she said, 'what was your name again?'

'Jack,' said Jack. 'Jack Stalwart,' he added.

'I don't remember Thomas ever mentioning your name. Do you and he go to school together?' she asked as she handed over the glass.

'No,' said Jack, 'we don't go to school together. But Thomas and I have a similar interest in dinosaurs.'

'Oh,' she said. 'You must be in that science club with him. Let me go and tell him you're here.'

She walked down the short hallway to the first door on the left and knocked twice. 'Thomas,' she said, leaning close to the door, 'your friend Jack from the science club is here to see you.'

A voice came from inside the room. 'I don't know any Jack.'

'Thomas Eberly,' she said, raising her voice, 'don't be rude! Now you come out here and see your friend Jack. He's come all this way to visit you.'

There was a short pause. Something rustled inside the bedroom. Thomas came out of his bedroom, quickly closing the door behind him. He walked down the hallway towards Jack, who was standing in the kitchen. Thomas, with his red hair and freckles, stood there looking absolutely fine. He didn't look sick at all.

'See,' said his mum, pointing to Jack, 'Jack has come to see you.'

'I don't know this kid, Mom,' said Thomas as he stared at Jack. Mrs Eberly looked over at Jack with a confused expression.

'No,' said Jack. 'Thomas and I haven't met before. I am here on behalf of the Global Protection Force to collect something he took that doesn't belong to him.'

Jack pulled out the picture from his pocket and showed it to Thomas.

Thomas looked at it and then looked at Jack. 'Where did you get this?' he asked.

'Don't worry about that,' said Jack. 'What's important is that you return what you took.'

Mrs Eberly looked even more confused. 'What is this all about, Thomas?' she asked.

Just then a loud crash came from the direction of Thomas's bedroom. Then there was a series of barks.

Thomas looked at Jack. 'That's just my dog, Freddie,' he said, quickly dismissing the noise. 'He's just playing in my room.' He turned to his mum. 'Mom,' he went on, answering his mum's earlier question, 'I didn't steal anything. I only borrowed it,' he said, trying to make a distinction.

'Thomas,' said his mum, growing concerned. 'What did you take?'

An even bigger crash came from the bedroom now. Then a loud bang, as if something had hit a wall, hard.

'Look, Mom,' explained Thomas, 'I only borrowed a small piece of bone from the

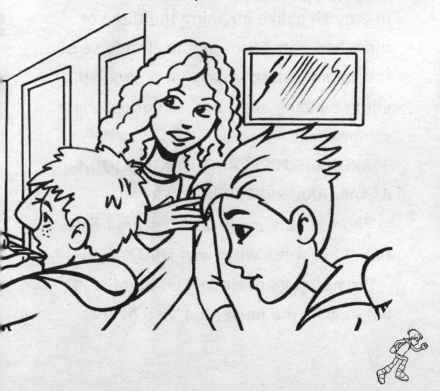

Museum of Natural History yesterday. I was going to return it when I was finished with my science project.'

'Thomas Richard Eberly,' said the boy's mother angrily, 'I can't believe you took something that didn't belong to you. You should know better!'

'GRRRRR . . . GRRRRR . . .' Growling sounds were coming from Thomas's room. Then, out of nowhere, the growl changed to a noise unlike anything the three of them had ever heard before. The force of the sound was so great that it shook the entire building and almost knocked them off their feet.

'RRRRRRRRRRRRRROOOOOOOOOOOOO-AAAAAAAAARRRRRRRRRRRRRR!'

'Thomas!' his mum yelled, scared half out of her wits. 'What was THAT?'

Thomas gulped. He looked frightened not only by the noise, but also by the

inevitable scolding he was going to get from his mum.

The sound came booming from the room again.

'RRRRRRRRRRRRRROOOOOOOOOOOOO-AAAAAAAAAARRRRRRRRRRRRRRR!'

Thomas's eyes darted towards his room. 'Um,' he said nervously, 'that's this year's science project, Mom.'

CRASH! There was a splintering noise from Thomas's bedroom.

'RRRRRRRRRRRRRROOOOOOOOOOOOO-AAAAAAAAAARRRRRRRRRRRRRRR!'

Jack looked quickly round the corner.

Whatever it was had blown Thomas's door clear out of its frame. All that was left was thousands of wooden splinters strewn across the carpet in the hallway. Jack could hear something moving. He waited to see what it was.

Slowly, an enormous green head lowered itself through what used to be the doorway, and into the hallway. It was so massive that it barely fitted through the door frame. Its eyes, which were black and bulging, were roaming up and down the hall. The hundreds of teeth that lined its wide jaws were tall, thin and razor-sharp.

It was hungry, Jack thought, not only because it was drooling, but also because it seemed to be sniffing for prey. Based on the size of the head alone, Jack reckoned that the creature was about a metre taller than a fully grown man.

'RRRRRRRRRRRRROOOOOOOOOOOOO-
AAAAAAAAARRRRRRRRRRRRRR!'

Its fearsome roar made Jack jump.
Although he hadn't yet seen its body, Jack
recognized the head from Lewis Porter's
book. It was the head of the most
ferocious carnivore of the Late Jurassic. It
was the allosaurus. And Thomas had
brought it to life in his very own bedroom.

Chapter 8:
The Escape

'Underneath the kitchen table!' Jack screamed as he yanked Thomas and his mum out of the creature's sight.

'RRRRRRRRRRRRRROOOOOOOOOOOOO-AAAAAAAAARRRRRRRRRRRRRRR!'

The frame around Thomas's bedroom door came down with a crash. There wasn't much time. The dinosaur had broken through and was walking on its hind legs down the Eberlys' hallway. It seemed to be growing by the second.

THUD. THUD. THUD. It was coming closer.

SNIFF. SNIFF. It was trying to pick up their scent.

From their hiding place, Jack reached into his Secret Agent Book Bag and pulled out a can of Neutralizing Spray. The GPF's Neutralizing Spray got rid of any scent, whether human or animal. Perfect protection, Jack thought, against meat-

eating dinosaurs. Jack quickly sprayed himself, Thomas and Mrs Eberly, just as the dinosaur made its way to the kitchen. Mrs Eberly was trying very hard not to scream.

Jack risked a look from underneath the tablecloth. The allosaurus hadn't smelled a thing. It moved past them towards the front door.

THUD. THUD. THUD. It looked as if it knew where it was going.

CRASH! It slammed against the front door, knocking it down. BLAM! It thundered down the hallway outside and broke through the main entrance, then made its way out onto the street.

'RRRRRRRRRRRRROOOOOOOOOOOOO-AAAAAAAAAARRRRRRRRRRRRRR!'

From where they were hiding, Jack could hear the screams of frightened New Yorkers as they encountered the unbelievable sight of a dinosaur running towards them. Mrs Eberly's eyes were wide with shock. She couldn't speak. Thomas had brought back to life one of the most ferocious dinosaurs in history. And now it was loose on the streets of New York City.

Chapter 9:
The Hope

Once the dinosaur had left the building, Thomas jumped out from beneath the table.

'WOW!' he exclaimed. 'I can't believe I did it! I turned my dog, Freddie, into a living, breathing allosaurus! All I had to do was isolate the dinosaur's DNA from the toe bone, mix it with a quickening solution and give it to Freddie. The transformation was almost instantaneous. No one has ever been able to extract DNA from dinosaur fossils. I'm definitely going to win first prize now!'

'Are you crazy?' Mrs Eberly shouted. 'That thing could have killed us! You should be ashamed of yourself for not thinking of the damage it will cause!'

Thomas looked at his mum and then at Jack, both of whom were wearing grave expressions.

'I'm sorry,' said Thomas, looking sheepishly at the ground. He was starting to regret what he'd done. 'Am I grounded?'

'Grounding you isn't punishment enough!' his mother yelled. 'I'm sure the police'll be knockin' on our door when they find out it was you who created this . . . this . . . THING!'

Thomas looked pale. 'If it helps,' he offered, holding up a vial with clear fluid inside, 'I developed a reversal serum that will change the dinosaur back into Freddie. We just need to get close enough to make him drink it.'

Jack quickly grabbed the reversal serum out of Thomas's hand.

'Right,' he said, 'I'll take this and give it to the allosaurus. You stay here,' he told Thomas. 'I'll call you when it's safe to join me.'

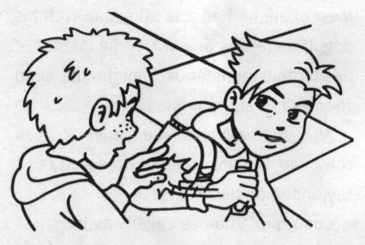

'You mean I can't come?' said Thomas, trying to make Jack feel bad. 'After all, it's my dog, Freddie, that's trapped inside that monster.'

Jack thought for a second about what to do. He wondered whether Max had ever taken a civilian with him on one of his missions. Bringing someone who wasn't a secret agent was always a risky thing to do. But bringing Thomas, Jack reasoned, could be a good thing. Thomas knew New York City better than Jack. He also probably knew more about the allosaurus. Most of all, he had a relationship with his dog. If there was any of Freddie inside this terrible monster, Jack might just need Thomas to help him out.

'All right,' said Jack reluctantly. 'You can come too, but you need to do exactly as I say and stick close to me.'

'Cool!' said Thomas eagerly as he bounded towards the hole in the wall that used to be his front door.

'Y'all be careful, OK?' said Mrs Eberly, looking concerned.

'Don't worry,' said Jack, trying to reassure her. 'Thomas is in good hands. I won't let anything happen to him.'

Mrs Eberly sighed and then smiled. Jack nodded to her and raced out of the apartment. Then Thomas gave his mum a big hug and dashed out behind Jack. In the distance, a huge roar sounded out across the city.

Chapter 10:
The First Encounter

Jack and Thomas bolted down the steps
and onto the pavement. Jack looked to
the left and then to the right, but there
was no sign of the dinosaur anywhere.
The only indication that the dinosaur
existed were the huge pieces of glass
strewn everywhere from when it had burst
out of the Eberlys' building and onto the
street.

Suddenly there was a loud roar. The
dinosaur was still close by.

'Quick!' said Jack to Thomas. 'We need
to get the reversal serum into the

allosaurus before it's too late!'

Jack and Thomas dashed round the corner and onto 34th Street. In the middle of the road was the dinosaur. It was frantically swooping down as it ran in an attempt to gobble up people before they could get away. They were screaming as they fled from the monstrous creature.

'Help us!' yelled a man.

'Don't hurt my baby!' shrieked a woman.

The boys raced towards the allosaurus. Up ahead, Jack noticed a man standing still on the pavement. It was as if he was too scared to run. The dinosaur noticed him too, and turned to walk in his direction. It began to stalk him step by step, and when it reached him it flashed its daggered teeth as if to say, 'Now I am going to eat you.'

'Help me!' yelled the man, to anyone who could hear him.

'Stay where you are and don't move!'
Jack shouted. Not that he was going
anywhere – the man's legs seemed to be
glued to the spot.

The dinosaur took a step back and then
forward again. It began to sniff the man

and stomp excitedly from side to side.

The only way Jack could save the man was to distract the dinosaur with the prospect of a tastier meal. Thinking quickly, he yanked the Virtual Projection Camera out of his Book Bag. Although it resembled a small video camera, it could project images that looked and smelled like the real thing. Remembering Lewis Porter's book, he lifted up the camera and punched in the word 'camptosaurus'. Instantly a virtual image of the plant-eating dinosaur appeared on a white wall just a few metres from the frightened man.

The allosaurus stood up on its hind legs as soon as it smelled the camptosaurus. It quickly forgot about the man and began to stalk the other dinosaur. The monster bellowed at the camptosaurus and then opened its jaws wide before snapping them shut with a great big *CHOMP!* Its

front teeth hit the brick wall hard, sending one of them into the air and onto the pavement with a *CHINK!*

'That must have hurt,' said Thomas.

'RRRRRRRRRRRRROOOOOOOOOOOOOAA AAAAAAARRRRRRRRRRRRRRR!'

The allosaurus wasn't happy.

'You stay here,' said Jack to Thomas as he left Thomas's side and ran as fast as he could towards the man.

'Run!' Jack yelled, and he shoved the

man out of harm's way. The shock of
being pushed seemed to wake the man's
legs and he quickly dived into a
restaurant on the corner.

Jack stood there panting. He looked
over at Thomas, who was twenty metres
away. Thomas was trying to tell him
something. Jack squinted his eyes and
tried to read Thomas's lips. It looked as if
he was saying, 'Wash out.'

Just then, an awful smell wafted into
Jack's nose. It smelled like the stench of a
thousand rubbish bags that had been
sitting out in the sun all day. Slowly, Jack
turned and looked out of the corner of his
eye. He gasped in fright. The allosaurus
had snuck up behind him and was
breathing hot dinosaur breath all over
him. Instead of the man he had saved,
now *Jack* was face-to-face with the most
terrifying creature that he had ever seen.

'RRRRRRRRRRRRROOOOOOOOOOOOOAA-
AAAAAAARRRRRRRRRRRRRRR!'

Chapter 11:
The Goo

The dinosaur's powerful roar blew Jack off his feet and backwards onto the street. He landed on his back and hit his head hard on the tarmac. A throbbing pain shot through his skull and he wondered if he had actually cut it open. But thankfully he hadn't.

The dinosaur crept forward and leaned down towards Jack. *SNIFF. SNIFF.* It was trying to tell whether Jack was dead or not. Jack, even in his dazed state, knew that it was only a matter of time before the dinosaur attacked him. He needed to do something – and fast.

Jack gathered his wits and counted to three. He shut his eyes and rolled over twice, swiftly crawling to his knees. Keeping his gaze fixed on the allosaurus, he reached backwards into his Book Bag and pulled out a long tube. This was the GPF's Goo Tube – a perfect solution to Jack's current problem.

The Goo Tube had a glue-like substance hidden inside that, when ejected, expanded on impact. Usually Jack used the Goo Tube to plug holes. As the dinosaur's mouth was as good a hole as any, Jack lifted the tube to face the creature and pushed the ejector button. The expandable goo flew into the dinosaur's mouth, just as

it opened its jaws. *BLOOP! POP!* The goo
blew up in an instant so that the dinosaur
couldn't close its chops. There was no
way it could bite into Jack now. Jack
sprinted back to Thomas.

'That was close!' exclaimed Thomas.

'Thanks for the warning,' said Jack, giving Thomas a friendly slap on the back. Jack thought a bit better of Thomas for trying to help him. Maybe he was all right after all.

Jack and Thomas dashed into a nearby launderette and looked at the dinosaur through the glass front door. With the sound of tumble dryers and washing machines rumbling in the background, Jack watched as the dinosaur rapidly ate through the goo. It smacked its lips and then headed further along 34th Street.

'What's up ahead?' Jack asked Thomas.

'The Empire State Building,' said Thomas, looking worried.

Jack knew that the Empire State Building was one of the most famous buildings in New York City. Hundreds of people usually waited outside to get into the building and up to the observation deck, and the dinosaur was headed straight for them. How was he going to save so many people at once?

Jack thought about his brother Max and the advice Max used to give him.

'A successful secret agent,' Max used to say, 'clears his mind first and then thinks of a plan.'

Jack did exactly as Max told him. He took a deep breath and considered the risky situation ahead. Almost immediately, an idea popped into his brain.

'Got it!' he said to himself, pleased that he'd come up with a way to distract the monster. Now it was time to put his plan into action, before the dinosaur ate its first victim.

Chapter 12:
The Dreamy World
of Biscuits

Jack turned to Thomas.

'Do you have any dog biscuits on you?' he asked.

'Huh?' said Thomas, with a confused expression on his face. 'Um. Yeah, I do,' he answered.

'Great,' said Jack. 'Let me have them.'

Thomas rifled through his trouser pockets and pulled out a half-eaten bag of dog biscuits. He handed it to Jack, who threw it on the ground and began to stamp all over it.

Thomas scratched his head, wondering what on earth Jack was up to.

'Perfect,' said Jack as he picked up the bag of dog-biscuit dust. 'Just what I need. Let's get going.'

Jack shoved open the launderette door and raced down the street towards the allosaurus, with Thomas following close behind. Up ahead, as Jack had expected, there was a queue of people waiting to enter the Empire State Building. The dinosaur was running their way.

'RRRRRRRRRRRRRROOOOOOOOOOOOO-AAAAAAAAARRRRRRRRRRRRRR!'

It announced its presence. The terrified people turned and started squealing.

Jack reached into his Book Bag. He pulled out the Spray Gun and grabbed an empty vial that was clipped to its side. Then he poured the dog-biscuit dust into the tube and inserted it into the gun. He closed the latch and pointed it into the sky ahead of the dinosaur. Jack pulled the trigger and a spray of biscuit dust was ejected to the right of the dinosaur's path.

As soon as it smelled the biscuits, the allosaurus stopped in its tracks. It looked as if there was a bit of Freddie in it after all! Its enormous tail was wagging excitedly and it dreamily began to run right into the biscuit dust and away from the queue of people. Freddie the dinosaur was sniffing in all the biscuit vapours he could.

Quickly, Jack and Thomas ran towards the terrified people and hurried them into a nearby department store. From inside the store,

they watched the allosaurus stand up. It
shook its head and came out of the
trance. The dinosaur looked around to
find no one left on the street. Just like a
dog, it cocked its leg on a nearby fire
hydrant and then carried on along 34th
Street until it hit Broadway, where it
moved north.

Jack pulled out his map of New York City. It looked as though the dinosaur was heading towards 42nd Street and Times Square, one of the most populated places in the city. They were at least ten blocks away from Times Square. There was no way that he and Thomas could keep up with the allosaurus for ten blocks. They needed help. They needed the Flyboard.

Chapter 13:
The Flyboard

Jack ran outside. He reached into his
Book Bag and pulled out the GPF's
Flyboard, which was one of the newer
gadgets in the GPF's arsenal. It looked
like a skateboard only it had two small
hydrogen-powered jets mounted on the
back. He unfolded the board so it clicked
into place, put it on the ground and
stepped on.

'Hop on!' he shouted to Thomas.

Jack punched the 'wheels' button on his
Watch Phone and activated the 'wheels'
feature. Before he knew it, the jet engines

fired up and he and Thomas were speeding towards the dinosaur that was now at least six blocks ahead.

'RRRRRRRRRRRRROOOOOOOOOOOOO-AAAAAAAAARRRRRRRRRRRRRRR!'

Jack could see the allosaurus in front of them. It was within minutes of reaching Times Square.

'Get inside!' he screamed to the people up ahead. 'Get inside!' But Jack was too far away for anyone to hear him.

'I have to warn them!' he shouted

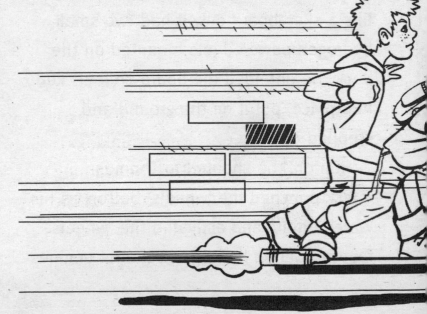

to Thomas above the noise of the Flyboard's jet engines. He scrambled through his Book Bag and reached for the Warning Gun. Quickly he lifted it up and looked at the side of the barrel. There were twenty-six buttons on the Warning Gun, one for each letter of the alphabet.

He punched in the phrase D-A-N-G-E-R-G-E-T-I-N-D-O-O-R-S, pointed the barrel into the air and pulled the trigger. The letters shot up one by one like puffs of smoke, so that the message could be seen all over the city. 'That should do it,' said Jack, smiling at his quick thinking. He hooked the Warning Gun onto one of the belt loops on his trousers in case he needed it again.

The Flyboard meant they were catching up with the dinosaur. They sailed past 39th and 40th Streets, heading towards 42nd Street and Times Square.

'RRRRRRRRRRRRRROOOOOOOOOOOOO-
AAAAAAAAARRRRRRRRRRRRRRR!'

The dinosaur announced itself as it
entered Times Square. Jack and Thomas
zoomed in just behind it. There were giant
television screens flickering on the tops of
buildings. Cars were pulled to the side of
the road with their doors open and no
one left inside. Everyone must have seen
Jack's message. Jack was pleased. The
dinosaur looked disgusted.

'RRRRRRRRRRRRRROOOOOOOOOOOOO-
AAAAAAAAARRRRRRRRRRRRRRR!'

In its rage, the dinosaur trampled over
several yellow New York taxis. CRUNCH!
PING! The sound was almost deafening as
metal and glass flew all over the road.
Jack and Thomas ducked to avoid the
spewing debris. When the noise stopped,
Jack and Thomas lifted their heads. The
dinosaur was running north again,

towards the upper parts of the city.

'Where do you think it's headed?' Jack asked Thomas.

'Well, if it was Freddie,' said Thomas, 'probably Central Park.'

'Why Central Park?' asked Jack.

'Because,' Thomas explained, 'Freddie loves to visit the animals at the Central Park Zoo.'

Jack thought for a minute. It made even more sense that the allosaurus would be heading for the zoo. The animals were mainly kept in cages so they would be easy prey. There would be no way they could escape the dinosaur's powerful jaws. And, of course, they couldn't read Jack's message. They would have no idea that a deadly dinosaur was headed their way.

'Quick!' said Jack. 'We have to save the animals!'

Jack fired up the Flyboard once again and he and Thomas jetted off, leaving only a light trail of water-filled steam behind them. They knew it was a race against time, and they had some catching up to do.

Chapter 14:
The Hero

Jack and Thomas sped towards the park. Up ahead, Thomas spotted the dinosaur. 'It's reached the park!' he screamed. The two of them watched as its swaying tail disappeared underneath the trees.

Jack and Thomas ducked as the Flyboard carried them under the same trees and onto a road. On the other side of the road was an enormous ice-skating rink. The dinosaur was already there and about to cross it.

'It's crossing the ice!' yelled Thomas as the dinosaur slammed through a glass barrier and stepped onto the cold, hard rink. Thankfully for Jack, the ice rink had just closed for the year, so there weren't any people around.

'RRRRRRRRRRRRROOOOOOOOOOOOO-AAAAAAAAARRRRRRRRRRRRRR!'

The allosaurus lumbered across the ice and made it to the other side. It roared again before picking up its feet and moving north, this time across the grass.

Jack and Thomas arrived at the edge of the ice and stopped. There was no way round the rink. They had to cross it too. Jack activated the 'blades' feature on the Flyboard. Instantly, the wheels were sucked inside and two long blades popped down. Jack fired up the jets and the Flyboard carried them across the ice at top speed, faster than any champion speed skater could skate.

As they reached the opposite side of

the rink, the Flyboard began to bleep.
Jack looked down. It was not an
encouraging noise. The power bar was
telling him that there was almost no
hydrogen left. There was no way the
Flyboard could carry them any further.
Jack needed to think of another way.

Quickly, he looked around. To his right,
parked on the road, was a yellow taxi with
a man inside. Jack dashed over to the taxi
and banged hard on the window. The

man, who was cowering inside, jumped in his seat and then peered out. He looked at Jack and reluctantly rolled down the window.

'I need a favour,' said Jack breathlessly. 'I need you to drive north on this road.'

'But, zee dinosaur is out zair!' screamed the man. 'I don't vant to be ee-ten!'

'I know,' said Jack. 'I am trying to capture him. If you help me, you'll be a hero.'

'A hee-ro?' said the man, a grin brimming on his face. He paused for a second and then said, 'OK, I vill help you.'

'Great!' said Jack. 'C'mon, get in!' he shouted to Thomas as he opened the passenger door of the taxi and dived into the back seat.

Thomas jumped in behind Jack. The taxi driver started the car and slammed his

foot on the pedal. The car screeched
north after the dinosaur and towards the
helpless animals that had no idea what
was coming their way.

Chapter 15:
The Dilemma

Jack looked out at the park from inside the moving car. In the distance, he could see the dinosaur running through the trees and over the ancient boulders that littered the grass. If it weren't for the taxi driver, Jack would have lost the dinosaur by now, but they were almost neck and neck with it and Jack felt sure that they would beat it to the zoo.

The road curved slightly to the left. 'Look!' said Thomas to Jack as he pointed to a building. 'That's the zoo.'

'Great,' said Jack. He leaned towards

the driver. 'Can you pull over here,
please?' he asked.

The driver veered to the left and
brought the car to a dead stop.

Jack flung open the door. 'Thanks!' he
yelled as he and Thomas bolted out of
the car and ran towards the entrance.

Jack and Thomas ran past a sign saying THE ZOO IS NOW CLOSED and jumped over the turnstiles. They dashed into the meeting area and looked around. The dinosaur was nowhere in sight. As far as Jack could tell, they had managed to beat it to the zoo.

Jack panted breathlessly and thought about the situation. Central Park was spread over 843 acres. The allosaurus could be anywhere. If Thomas was wrong about where Freddie was heading, Jack might fail in his mission. He had to trap the dinosaur and somehow administer the serum.

As Jack was thinking about what to do, he heard a sound. It was the dinosaur's roar and it was coming their way.

Chapter 16:
The Transformation

Jack told Thomas to run for cover while he prepared for the allosaurus to arrive. He quickly reached into his Book Bag and grabbed a metal canister. Inside the container was another GPF gadget – the Rubber Slide – but Jack didn't need the slide today, just the canister itself. He stood there, with the canister in his hands, and waited for the dinosaur to enter the zoo.

'RRRRRRRRRRRRRROOOOOOOOOOOOO-AAAAAAAAARRRRRRRRRRRRRRR!'

The dinosaur ripped through the

entrance and smashed the turnstiles. It raged into the meeting area where Jack was standing and paused for a second while it registered his presence. Jack stood there, his knees beginning to tremble.

Slowly, the dinosaur pawed its way over to Jack and lowered its head. It took a long sniff at Jack and showed him its razor-sharp teeth. A drip of drool slid off one of its teeth and splattered onto Jack's foot. All Jack needed was for the dinosaur to roar again and his plan could be put into action.

'RRRRRRRRRRRRROOOOOOOOOOOO-AAAAAAAAARRRRRRRRRRRRRR!'

With one swift toss, Jack hurled the canister in the direction of the dinosaur's gaping mouth. The metal cylinder wedged itself at the back of the allosaurus's jaws, making it impossible for the dinosaur to close its gob. The creature stood up and shook its head violently, trying to loosen the canister.

Quickly, Jack pulled the reversal serum out of his trouser pocket and the Super Sling out of his Book Bag. He placed the vial into the catapult and pulled it as far back as he could. With trembling hands he aimed the vial directly at the dinosaur's mouth and fired. *TWANG!*

The serum shot through the air and landed right on the dinosaur's tongue. As it shook its head, the glass vial slipped underneath the metal can and down the back of the creature's throat. The serum was now inside its stomach and it was only a matter of time before it started to work. Jack and Thomas stared at the goings-on with horror and hope.

Suddenly, the dinosaur bolted upright as if it had been frozen solid. Jack

watched as it swayed to the right and
then to the left before crashing down to
the ground with an incredible *THUD!*

It lay there for only a moment before an
enormous gust of wind blew in from the

east. The violent wind swirled around the allosaurus and began to turn its bones to dust. Jack, his eyes wide as saucers, watched as a second gust of wind came from the west and carried the dinosaur dust away in a big *WHOOSH!*

When Jack looked down again, all that
was left was his metal canister, a toe
bone and a cute little dog that was
wagging its tail excitedly at the animals
across the meeting area.

'Freddie!' Thomas shouted with joy as he
ran over to his beloved pet. 'I'm so glad
you're alive! Thanks to Jack, you're back!'

Freddie licked Thomas's face, then
when Jack leaned down to the dog
Freddie licked him too.

In the distance, Jack could hear the
sounds of police sirens. They were
coming to capture the dinosaur.

Jack thought about how shocked
they would be to find that it had
completely vanished.

He turned to Thomas, who was
stroking Freddie's fur. 'You know,'
he said to Thomas, 'there's still
something you need to do.'

'I know,' said Thomas, looking a bit sheepish. 'I need to return the toe bone. Can we do it together?' he asked Jack. 'I'm a bit nervous.'

'Sure,' said Jack as he and Thomas stood up.

Jack collected his canister and put the ancient bone safely in his pocket. Then the three of them – Jack, Thomas and Freddie – made their way west out of the park and towards the museum.

Chapter 17:
The Apology

The trio climbed the steps of the museum and walked inside. There, atop a ladder, dusting the dinosaur bones, was Lewis Porter.

'Hi, Lewis,' said Jack as he and Thomas walked towards him.

Lewis turned round. 'Hi, Jack!' he said excitedly, clambering down the ladder. 'Any luck? I heard about the commotion on the news. I was tempted to get out onto the streets and see the action for myself, but knowing these dinosaurs as well as I do, I decided to stay indoors.

'You were right to do that,' said Jack. 'It was a pretty hairy situation. But we got it under control and we – that is, Thomas and I – have something to return.'

He pulled the missing toe bone out of his pocket, gave it to Thomas and nudged him forwards. 'Thomas, here,' Jack said, 'has something to say.'

'Um . . . Um . . .' Thomas said, looking sheepishly at the ground. 'I just wanted to say that I am sorry for taking the bone. I shouldn't have done it. I made a mess of everything. I created a monster that could have killed people. I feel awful.'

Lewis didn't say anything. He let Thomas carry on.

'And, well, anyway,' added Thomas, 'I'd like to repay you by helping out here at the museum. That is, if you'd let me.'

Lewis took a few seconds to think and then smiled at Thomas. 'Wonderful,' he

said. 'I could use the help. The police might even look more kindly on you if they know you're making amends. Why don't you start by dusting the dinosaurs?' Lewis suggested. 'You can begin at the top,' he said, pointing to an incredibly tall ladder, 'at the head of the barosaurus.'

Thomas looked at the barosaurus and gulped. 'You know,' he said nervously, 'um . . . I'm a bit scared of heights.'

Lewis looked at Thomas. A grin spread across his face.

'Well, I guess I'd better be going,' Jack said to them. He turned to Thomas and smiled. 'Take care of yourself, Thomas. And Freddie too,' he said as he patted Freddie's head.

'Sure will,' said Thomas. 'Thanks again,' he said. 'Without your help I don't know what would have happened. I've definitely learned my lesson.' He looked a bit sad to see Jack go.

Jack smiled and turned to Lewis. 'Are there any maps of the world around here?' he asked.

'Of course,' Lewis answered. 'Through the main hall and to the left.'

Jack said goodbye and walked further into the museum, leaving Thomas to clamber up the ladder, his knees clearly shaking with fear.

After Jack passed by some other exhibits in the museum, he noticed the map of the world that Lewis was talking about. Not as big as his own, mind you, but it would do.

He pulled out a small flag from his Book Bag and stuck it into the map on top of Britain. Instantly, a light began to glow inside the country.

Jack waited for the light to shine brightly before he shouted, 'Off to England!' It flickered and burst, sucking Jack into the map and transporting him home.

Chapter 18:
The Last Look

When Jack arrived, he found himself in
the middle of his room. The time on the
clock was exactly 7:31 p.m. Suddenly he
remembered something.

'Now where are they?' Jack asked
himself as he rummaged through the
clothes in the middle drawer of his chest
of drawers.

When he spied what he was looking for
he pulled them out. After a quick change,
he walked over to his full-length mirror
and took a good look. There he was,
dressed head to toe in the dinosaur

pyjamas that he'd got for Christmas. There were all sorts of dinosaur images on his PJs, but the one on his shoulder was definitely a picture of an allosaurus.

'A perfect end to this mission,' he said, smiling to himself as he walked over to his bed and crawled under the covers.

''Night, Whizzy,' he said to his miniature globe. Then he turned out the light and fell asleep.

SECRET AGENT

JACK STALWART

The Mystery
of the
Mona Lisa:
FRANCE

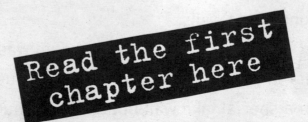

Read the first
chapter here

Chapter 1:
The Vanishing Lady

The museum in Paris had been closed for
several hours and the Bon Homme
cleaning crew were busy at work. Over a
hundred cleaners were scurrying through
the huge museum, mopping the floors
and dusting the railings, taking care not
to damage the precious paintings that
hung on its walls.

One of the rooms in the museum was
known as the '*Mona Lisa* room', because
on a special fake wall in the middle hung
the most famous painting in the world.

The *Mona Lisa* was a painting of a woman clothed in a brown dress with a mysterious smile on her face. It was painted over four hundred years ago by an artist named Leonardo da Vinci. It was so valuable that the museum had invested in a bullet-proof-glass security box, which was fixed over the painting to protect it from anyone who wanted to do it harm.

On this night, Hélène, one of Bon Homme's senior cleaners, made her way to the *Mona Lisa* room. As usual, she entered the room after her assistant, Jean Paul, had mopped the floor. She walked over to the glass box with the *Mona Lisa* inside and pulled out a special dusting cloth. She lifted the cloth and tried to wipe over it. But something was wrong. The front of the box was no longer there.

Hélène blinked twice and then let out a

piercing scream that shook the entire
room. 'The *Mona Lisa* is gone!' she
screamed. 'The world's most famous
painting has been stolen from the
Louvre!'